Fearless

Soulshifter Book 1

By

Shéa MacLeod

Cover Art: Amanda Kelsey

Formatting: PyperPress

Thanks as always to my critique partners, beta readers, and editors who make every book so much better

Thanks to B. T. for sharing her expertise on addictions and recovery. Any inaccuracies in that department are mine.

Please visit Shéa MacLeod at sheamacleod.wordpress.com

Acknowledgments

A big thank you as always to my friends at The Eclective:

Alan Nayes
M Edward McNally
Heather Marie Adkins
Tara West
Emma Jameson
RG Porter
Christine DeMaio-Rice
Greg James

***

This one's for Lyn

Shéa MacLeod

CHAPTER ONE

Ms. Higgins slid a copy of Bram Stoker's *Dracula* onto the shelf and heaved a sigh. Finally. She could go home. It was late and it had been one of *those* days. Sometimes she wondered what had possessed her to become a high school librarian.

Smoothing a wayward strand of gray hair back where it belonged, she made her way carefully through the deep shadows cast by the stacks. Most people would have left all the overhead lights on instead of just the ones at the front, but Ms. Higgins was not most people. No sense in wasting energy. She didn't need that much light to work. She knew where every book went. After all, she'd been at this for nearly forty years.

Her sensible heels suddenly slid out from under her. Arms flailing, she shrieked as she collapsed in a heap on the ground, face pressed to the rough carpet. Her wrist gave a painful twinge. That was all she needed: an injury right before she planned to paint her dining room.

Ms. Higgins started to get up, but something under her cheek was wet and slippery. Sitting up cautiously, she frowned as she swiped her hand at the wetness on her face. As she stared at dark stuff coating her hand, the coppery tang finally registered: blood.

Scrambling to her feet, she slid again, this time careening sideways and landing on somebody's lap. A very dead somebody. Ms. Higgins opened her mouth and screamed and screamed and screamed.

CHAPTER TWO

"Please, please, please let me be me."

I stood in front of the bathroom mirror, eyes squeezed shut, as I'd done every morning since that cold February day a couple months ago. I clenched my fists at my sides willing today to be different. Taking a deep breath I opened my eyes.

"Shit."

"Abigail Evangeline Roberts. That is no way for a young lady to talk." The voice was muffled through the bathroom door, but my aunt's - or rather *her* aunt's - snippy tone was crystal clear.

"Sorry, Aunt Liz," I called through the door. "Broke a nail." Yeah. That was a good answer. Humans swore over silly things like broken nails all the time.

Aunt Liz said something about not being late, but I had already tuned her out. I had more important things to worry about than being late to some stupid school. Like the fact that the face staring back at me from the mirror wasn't mine. Like the fact I was wearing the skin of a dead girl.

Like the fact I was dead. Sort of.

The djinn couldn't technically die. Our only true physical form was what humans would mistake for a demon and it was immortal. Technically, we were beings made of pure energy capable of taking the form of anything we wished, but the form taking made us vulnerable. If our temporary form was killed, our energies became untethered from all of djinn. If that happened, we might as well be dead.

That is what had happened to me. My temporary physical form had been killed, my energy set free to roam. Without being tethered to the djinn, it had found a new home. A human one. I'd gone from being Zipporah - Zip to my friends - to Abbie, literally overnight. It was…unsettling.

There had been no point contacting my people, letting them know I was alive. According to djinn tradition, I was dead to the clan. This was my new life. Even if I could get in touch with them, which would be difficult seeing as how they lived in the middle of nowhere slightly out of phase with the rest of the world, they wouldn't accept me as djinn. Not while I was stuck in a human body.

I could have called Morgan Bailey, the local vampire hunter. We'd become friends while she was investigating a murder. But what could she do? Force the djinn to take me back? Return me to my former state? Not even she had the power to do that.

"Abbie, hurry up. I don't want to be late."

"Coming, Aunt Liz."

Abbie, that was the new me. A Miss Goody-Goody with a perfect attendance record and a four-point-oh, whatever that was. But Abbie had also had a secret dark side and an attitude problem a mile long. Of course, her aunt was the principal of the school, which was sort of like being the marid of a djinn clan, I guess. That explained both the overachiever thing and the attitude.

Frustration boiled up inside me. Anger, grief, fear all welling up to the breaking point. I had always wanted to know what it was like to be human, but not like this. I hated being stuck in this life I'd found myself in, and yet I had no choice but to carry on living it. Lost. Confused. Alone. Forever separated from my own kind.

I let out a sigh. That was one of the things about being human. All the feelings got so...crazy. Sometimes I thought my head would explode.

"Abbie, *now.*"

Flinging open the bathroom door, I shot Aunt Liz a scowl. "I'm coming. Give me a freaking minute."

She seemed startled by my outburst - apparently the real Abbie had been less volatile - but gave me a brief nod. "I'll be in the car." She turned and strode down the hall, her three inch lime-green heels making snappy little clicks on the wood floors.

With a shake of my head I hurried to my room to slip on my black ballet flats and grab my book bag. Another day of endless, boring frustration, annoying students, and condescending teachers. If only they knew that I wasn't an eighteen year old girl with an attitude problem, but a ten-thousand-year-old djinni.

Okay, I'd give them the attitude problem.

#

School was tedious. The resulting homework even more tedious. Perhaps most tedious of all was sitting at the dinner table with the woman who was supposed to be my aunt. Poor woman. She didn't appear to know what to do with me.

I stabbed a piece of greenery of dubious origin and eyeballed it. It looked disgusting. I took a delicate sniff. It smelled worse. She expected me to eat this *kuchra*?

"Abbie, would you stop playing with the broccoli and eat it?"

I took a delicate nibble of the green stuff and nearly spit it out. Was she trying to kill me? "I don't like it." I went for petulant teenager. I figured it fit well enough. By all accounts, Abbie had developed something of a bratty attitude after being dumped by her parents. Couldn't say I blamed her.

"You know what Dr. Neal said. You need iron. That's why you passed out and ended up in the hospital."

That was not why I, or rather Abbie, had passed out. Abbie had died. Dead as a doornail thanks to a tiny little thing in her brain called an aneurysm. The only reason Abbie's body was up walking around was because when I'd taken up residence in her empty shell, my djinn energy had healed the damage to her brain while at the same time retaining enough of her memories for me to function as Abbie Roberts. The memories came and went in bits and pieces: names of friends (Abbie hadn't had any to speak of), likes and dislikes (her thoughts on broccoli were similar to mine), bits about school. It was fuzzy and hard to access sometimes, but it was there. Still, I wasn't about to mention any of that to Aunt Liz.

"Isn't there a better way to get iron?"

Her normally pinched expression grew even more so. "If you think I'm buying you steaks like your parents did, you've got another thing coming, young lady."

I hated when she called me "young lady" in that snide tone of hers. It had become clear to me that Abbie's aunt held a great deal of resentment toward Abbie's parents and their financial status. Or, rather, formal financial status. But instead of sniping back, I kept my tone dry and even. "I was thinking more along the lines of supplements." I actually had no idea what a supplement was, but something told me it was the right thing to say. Or rather, what Abbie would have said.

"You want them, you can get a job and buy them." Aunt Liz pushed away from the table. "I expect you to finish your broccoli and then do the dishes." She started to walk away, but paused, her slim body hesitating in the doorway. "And get to bed early. I do not want a repeat of this morning."

"Sure."

I watched her stride away, her body rigid, back ramrod straight. I shook my head. As my friend, Morgan Bailey, would say, the woman needed to get laid. Good luck with that.

It wasn't that Liz Roberts was a bad looking woman, especially for her late forties. She was actually fairly attractive in a Michelle Pfeiffer kind of way, with hardly any lines or wrinkles. She was blond and blue-eyed, much like my new body. Or at least like my new body became after I dyed Abbie's mousy brown hair.

The problem was she always walked around like she had a stick up her backside and had been sucking on lemons. I guess if I had to deal with teenagers all day I'd look like that, too.

Oh, wait. I did have to deal with teenagers all day.

Needless to say, the green stuff did not get eaten. It went straight into the garbage disposal. I also did the decent thing and put the dishes in the dishwasher without having to be asked twice. I figured Liz deserved a break. After all, she was putting a roof over my head and food in my mouth while Abbie's parents were running around Africa saving what they referred to as "heathens." I admit I don't know much about Africa, but I'm pretty sure they're neither heathen nor in need of saving. Still, I'm not sure what I would have done if I'd have ended up in some other body besides Abbie's. There probably wouldn't have been an Aunt Liz taking care of me. I might even have been forced to get a real job.

Perish the thought. I mean, what on earth would a djinni do in the human world? I had zero skills. I couldn't even boil an egg properly.

No. For now I needed Liz and the safety and security of a roof over my head even if it meant going to school and doing chores.

Tossing the dishrag into the sink, I headed toward the stairs. Homework was done and I had no intention of going to bed early. I'd become addicted to British television thanks to Aunt Liz's Netflix subscription. Number Ten is my favorite. Just saying.

Halfway up the stairs I heard Liz's cell phone ringing. Not her personal cell phone either. The one she used for the school. I have no idea what made me do it. I didn't generally have a habit of spying on Abbie's aunt, but I crept back down the stairs toward the open living room door.

"Principal Roberts."

There was silence for a moment while the other person spoke. "I'm sorry. Detective who?"

Another pause followed by a slight gasp from Liz. "Is this a joke?"

More silence. "Do you…" she cleared her throat and it sounded like she was on the verge of tears. "Do you know who it was?"

Interesting. Clearly something had happened down at the school, but why were the police calling? Why not one of the school custodians? Or the rent-a-cops?

"Okay. I'll be right down. Shall I come straight to the library or…? Oh, all right. Yes. Yes."

I wasn't exactly the type to hang out in libraries so I couldn't imagine what on earth would have happened in one that required police involvement. Or why they would need the principal to come down in the middle of the night. A break in, maybe? But why on earth would anyone want to steal from a high school library?

Senior prank, maybe. I might be in the Senior class, but I had little interest in the activities of my so-called peers. Hard to relate to people who are not only thousands of years younger than you, but have no idea that any sentient species other than humanity exists on this planet.

I heard the faint beep of Liz hanging up her cell phone and hustled back up the stairs. I darted into my room and dove for the bed, grabbing a random schoolbook on the way. Moments later there was a knock on my bedroom door and Liz popped her head in. Her hair was sort of messy like she'd run her hands through it and her eyes were a bit red. Almost as if she'd been crying. Holy *infernus,* what was going on?

"Hey, Abbie, I need to go out for a bit."

"Something wrong, Aunt Liz?"

She gave me a weak smile. "Nothing to worry about."

Lie. I could almost smell it. "Okay."

"I'll be back as soon as I can."

"Sure." I gave her a slight nod and went back to pretending to study my book.

Liz closed the door with a slight click. I waited until I heard her footsteps retreating down the stairs. Hearing the sound of the front door shutting behind her, I jumped off the bed and ran for my closet. I shoved my feet into a pair of navy Chucks, grabbed a jacket, and snatched my bag off the desk chair. Then I took my jewelry box off the dresser and dumped the contents on the bed, plucking a single key from amongst the assorted baubles.

I'd stumbled on the key one day shortly after taking possession of Abbie's body. The memory it sparked was one of Abbie angrily stealing Liz's school master key and having it copied. She'd done it after a particularly volatile confrontation with her aunt. Gods know what her plan had been. She'd never used it, losing her nerve the first time she tried to sneak into the empty school, but now it would come in handy.

I waited at the top of the stairs until I heard the car start, seeing the headlights as the car backed out of the driveway. Then I took the stairs two at a time, dashing down the hall, through the kitchen and into the garage.

There was a light layer of dust over the ugly gray bike. Really, I needed to do something about the color. But for now it would have to do.

I hurried back into the kitchen for the dish towel. Liz would kill me if she found out I used it to dust off my bike. I did it anyway.

I pushed the bike through the side door, locking it behind me, and rolled it down to the street. I eyed the thing dubiously. I decided then and there that being in a human body had finally driven me crazy. I was a ten thousand year old djinni who had never ridden a bike. Not a lot of need for it when one had teleportation skills. Unfortunately, those were gone along with most of the rest of my natural magic.

Still, I wanted desperately to know what had happened at the school. I had no idea why. Maybe because it was the most interesting thing that had happened to me since I'd become Abbie. Maybe...I don't know.

Still, I could do this. I could. Abbie had ridden a bike, so hopefully her body would remember how even if it was me running the show.

Squaring my shoulders, I threw one leg over the bike, straddling the thing just like I'd seen on television. Then with more guts than brains, I wobbled my way down the street.

CHAPTER THREE

I saw the red-and-blue strobe lights of the emergency vehicles long before I made it onto school grounds. The school wasn't far from home, and I managed to make it there in less than fifteen minutes without leaving too much skin on the asphalt.

I could make out five police cars, an ambulance, and Liz's SUV sort of angled around the front entrance. A small group of spectators huddled on the other side of the yellow-and-black crime tape strung haphazardly in front of the police cars.

I headed down the street that bordered the basketball courts to the west side of the school. There was only one police car there, blocking any thru traffic. The cop looked bored out of his mind. Anyone who wanted to get into the school could slip right past him quite easily. Like me, for instance.

Quickly stashing my bike in a clump of bushes, I continued on foot. This was an old neighborhood, the sidewalks lined heavily with shade trees. The branches, thick with spring leaves, effectively blocked out light from both the moon and the streetlights. I yanked the hood of my jacket up to cover the bright blond of my hair. The downside of the Marilyn Monroe look. But it was a look I'd favored for the last fifty odd years, and I had no intention of changing now. It was just trickier with an actual body to hone instead of magic to manipulate.

The police officer was clearly guarding not just the street, but the steps leading up from the sidewalk to the basketball courts. It was the only entrance to school grounds on this side of the building. At least, it was the only official one.

Keeping to deep shadows, I crept past the police car on the opposite side of the street. If I'd still been a djinni, this would have been easy. But I wasn't. All I could do was move with caution and hope like *infernus* the cop wouldn't see me.

He didn't.

Once I was a bit further down the street, I crossed over to the school side as quickly as I could. The cop didn't move, just leaned against his cruiser, checking his watch occasionally. Perfect.

At some point in the past, one groundskeeper or another had decided that a bare chain link fence around the school yard was far too institutional and bleak. So he, or she, had planted shrubs along the outside of the fence. I guess to give passersby something pretty to look at. It worked. The shrubbery softened the harsh lines of the fence, but it also allowed for something the groundskeeper probably hadn't expected: a way off the grounds without the teachers catching on.

Clever humans.

Using the shrubs to disguise their activities, past students had cut the fence in the thickest part of the shrubs. If one was reasonably careful, it was easy enough to slip in or out without anyone being the wiser. Mostly it was potheads, gangbangers, and other juvenile delinquents who used the escape hatch, though now and then other students used it as well. I myself had, once or twice, thanks to Abbie's memories.

I pushed my way carefully into the bushes and slipped through the gap in the fence. The basketball courts were completely deserted, the chain netting of the hoops making a *clink clink* as they swayed slightly in the breeze.

The side door to the school was locked up tight, but I had my ways. I pulled out the key I'd taken from my jewelry box and inserted it into the lock. It turned smoothly and I slipped inside the school.

The hallways on this side of the building were still dark, so I made my way carefully and silently through the corridors until I reached the one leading to the library. I poked my head around the corner slowly, lest anyone see.

Fluorescent lights cast a harsh glare over the hallway, empty but for a single police officer guarding the library's doorway. I ducked back around the corner. I wasn't going in that way. No surprise there. Fortunately, there were other ways into the library.

Slipping back outside, I made my way through the slightly damp grass to the side of the school where the library was located. Okay, yeah, I wasn't a library person, but Abbie had been a regular visitor. Sometimes to study. Most times to screw around without Liz breathing down her neck.

I eyed the narrow windows, picking one that would be behind the stacks out of sight of the main library area. One good solid shove and the cheap old lock snapped. Hopefully no one inside would notice.

Pushing the window open, I easily jumped up onto the sill and slipped into the room. Every light in the library was blazing, but the shelves kept me hidden from view.

The first thing that struck me was the coppery tang of blood mixed with the sickly sweet stench of death. After a few millennia, it was a scent I was familiar with. The smell turned my stomach. Somebody was not only dead, but had been that way for a few hours.

Moving silently through the stacks, I made my way toward the scent of blood and the sound of voices. Careful to stay out of the line of sight, I listened to the conversation.

"Jackson, why don't you take Ms. Higgins to the hospital? Stay with her a bit, make sure she's comfortable. Try and get a full statement if you can. Then you can go write up your report." I didn't recognize the voice, but I was pretty sure from the commanding tone he was the man in charge. "I'll stay here and wait for the coroner."

"Yes sir, Detective. Ms. Higgins?"

A detective? Based on what little I knew of human law enforcement thanks to shows like *CSI* and *Castle*, it made sense. What with there being a death and all. But what I wanted to know was if the death was due to suicide, accident, or something much more sinister.

My gut was telling me the latter.

There was a murmur from the school librarian, followed by some shuffling, then footsteps retreating from the room.

"Ms. Roberts?" It was the detective's voice. "Are you sure you want to stay here? Perhaps you should go with Ms. Higgins."

"No." Aunt Liz's tone was emphatic, though I detected a slight tremble beneath the bravado. "I'm the principal of this school and these children are my responsibility. I want to see the body."

A heavy sigh from the detective. "That's not our procedure, Ms. Roberts."

"You need someone to identify the, um, victim, is that correct?" Who knew Liz had such backbone?

"Usually that's done down at the morgue."

"Officially, yes," Liz agreed. "But unofficially, the earlier you know who it is, the faster you can figure out what happened."

Another sigh. "It's not pretty."

"Detective, I wrangle several hundred teenagers every day. I think I can handle not pretty."

"Alright. This way."

I could hear them moving closer, so I glanced around. The body was hidden from view by the stacks. As long as stayed where I was, they wouldn't be able to see me. Also, the officer on guard wouldn't be able to see the body from the doors, which meant I could check it out once Liz and the detective left.

"Do you know him?"

Liz made a little sound like a half-strangled sob. "Tim Newlund. He's a sophomore, I believe."

"Did you know him? Personally, I mean."

"Not really. He was one of those quiet sorts. Never really got into trouble, so I had no reason to see him in my office. I understand there was some bullying going on, though it didn't seem too severe. I allowed the teachers to deal with it. For the time being."

"He was a bully?" I could almost hear the censure in the detective's tone.

"No, no," Liz assured him. "He was being bullied." She cleared her throat. "I'm sorry, detective, this was a bit more than I expected. Is it alright if I get a cup of coffee? The teacher's lounge isn't far."

"I'll join you."

"But the body?"

"I'll leave a guard at the door."

I waited until I heard their footsteps echoing down the hall before I slipped from my hiding place. I stopped dead as I caught sight of the bloody scene. A boy sat slouched against the wall, a book bag beside him, skin pale and gray in death. His mouth and chin were coated in blood, almost as if he'd been drinking it, but he clearly wasn't a vampire. If he had been, there would have been nothing left of him but a pile of dust.

There was blood everywhere. It coated the front of his jacket and pooled around him in a slick puddle. The wall behind him was spattered with it like something out of one of those crime shows on TV. Arterial spray, I think they called it.

Crouching down next to the body, I took in every detail as fast as I could. I didn't recognize the boy, but that didn't mean anything. There were a lot of people at the school I didn't know. But still. He didn't deserve to die. Especially not this way.

His throat had been slashed ear to ear. It wasn't a smooth cut, either, but jagged like someone had taken a serrated blade to it. Or a dull hacksaw.

I studied his hands. Not a single mark on them. Nothing to indicate he'd struggled. I tipped his head forward slightly to check his skull for injury. As far as I could tell, there was no damage.

I glanced at the throat injury again. Something caught my eye and I leaned in closer. Almost obliterated by the slash were two very neat fang marks.

"*Kuchra.*"

They looked like vampire bites. But why would someone bite the kid and then slash his throat? It was like someone was trying to hide that this was a vampire attack. Except vamps didn't play that way. They didn't care if anyone found their kills. All they cared about was the blood. They would never cover up a bite like this.

Unless this wasn't about someone disguising a vampire attack as an ordinary murder. Maybe it was about someone trying to make an ordinary murder look like a vampire attack. Which was kind of stupid since only a few people in this country even knew vampires existed. If the cops noticed, they'd just chalk it up to those vampire wannabes roaming around these days.

But still, if it *was* somehow a vampire attack, I needed to know. I needed to stop it. This was my school now. My life. At least until I figured out how to free myself from this human body.

Besides, it was the perfect thing to keep my mind occupied. I could poke around. See what I can find out. No one would suspect me for a minute.

I heard voices from the hall. Somebody from the coroner's office, no doubt. My work here was done. For now. No point getting caught. I zipped across the room and out the window, closing it carefully behind me.

CHAPTER FOUR

The streets of Portland were still dark, the Craftsman-style houses silent and still. The occasional street light cast a mellow glow through the rising mist. It would be dawn soon, but for now I had the city to myself. More or less.

Before I'd been human, I wouldn't have even felt the night chill. As it was, I was glad for the jacket. It might be spring, but the nights could still be cold.

I figured Liz would be awhile yet, so I took my time wandering the quiet streets, past manicured lawns and well-trimmed hedges. My mind was a whirlwind. What should I do now? This wasn't my thing, really, this mystery-solving stuff, but I had to know. If there was a vampire or something on the loose, I needed to stop it.

Actually, what I needed to do was call the local vampire hunter, but what on earth would I say? "Hey Morgan, this is Zip. I'm human now. Surprise!"

Yeah. Right.

I could feel the maudlin thoughts seeping in. The longing for something that was gone. Maybe forever.

I gave myself a mental shake. *Come on, Zip. Focus.*

I shook my head. This was stupid. I had no idea what to do to even start an investigation. I had no special powers or skills. I was a high school student now, more's the pity. So I would do what a human would do. If a human knew about the supernatural. I would call the hunter.

I pulled out my cell and dialed a number from memory. "Please, pick up."

She didn't. It went straight to voicemail.

"Come on, Morgan. I need you." I punched in the number again. Still no answer.

Where was she? Why wasn't she answering?

A tone signaled I should leave my message. "Uh, hi. You don't know me, but my name is Abbie Roberts and we might have a problem at my school. You know, the kind of problem you deal with. Call me. Please." I hung up and shoved my phone back in my pocket.

I closed my eyes and inhaled deeply. "Okay, enough whining," I told myself sternly. If Morgan wasn't answering her phone, then I'd just go find her. The offices would be closed in the middle of the night, but she might be home if she wasn't out hunting. At the least I could maybe wait for her.

The first time I met Morgan Bailey she'd been trespassing onto djinn lands. She'd overpowered every system of protection we'd had in place. She was one of the most powerful people I'd ever met. I'd liked her instantly, although I don't think she appreciated me nearly as much.

But she'd cried when I died and that meant something. It meant even more that she'd comforted my marid. Tried to make him realize it hadn't been his fault. It had been that twit, Alberich. The Fairy Queen's crazy brother. He'd used the marid to kill me in order to try and start a war. Fortunately, Morgan figured it out and stopped the marid before a war could start. But not before he'd enacted his revenge on that freaking fairy, as Morgan used to call Alberich.

I had no idea if Morgan would believe I was Zip. Heck, I hardly believed it. But it didn't matter. I needed her. The school needed her.

Slipping past the bored cop, I rescued my bike from the bushes. I pedaled as fast as I could, headed for the Hawthorne District. It was a couple of miles away, but I figured I could get there in under an hour. Getting back before Liz came home was another matter. She was supposed to be working at her second job tonight, but with all that was going on at the school, she might decide to take the night off. Would she even notice I was gone? Mostly she just ignored me.

The marid had always noticed when I was gone. Even after ten thousand years, he still remembered everything there was to know about me. Except now I could never be part of that world again. My world.

Pushing back the sadness, I cut across the street and headed through the park, peddling so fast the trees blurred into a mass of almost solid green. More memories surfaced unbidden, flashing through my mind like a trailer of the saddest movie ever.

Snarling out a few choice curses, I squeezed out a little more speed. Maybe if I exhausted my body, my mind would stop remembering. I needed to forget what had been. At least for now.

I turned down Morgan's street. Her house was a small one-story bungalow. It was too dark to see what color it was. Something light. Maybe white or cream or lavender, knowing Morgan. A small brass lamp on the porch threw off just enough light to see the door was a rich eggplant purple. Definitely the right house.

Leaning my bike up against the house, I ascended to the porch. It was late, but Morgan was a night owl. The gentle bong of the doorbell shouldn't get her too out of sorts.

I stood there fidgeting, but no one answered the door. I rang three times just to be sure, then headed around to the back. Everything was dark. No sign of life.

Peering through the kitchen window I could just make out the unplugged coffee maker. She was gone for a while then. Morgan Bailey did not go anywhere without at least half a pot of coffee.

I leaned against the side of the house, trying to gather my thoughts. It wasn't easy. Abbie's memories came and went randomly. I never knew from one minute to the next if I'd remember something she'd done or said or experienced a year ago. My memories of before I was Abbie were sometimes hazy and vague. Like a dream. I easily forgot things. Things I, as Zip, should know. The only solid thing was the last two months since I became Abbie. I needed my memories and knowledge of the supernatural if I was going to figure this thing out.

I stared up at the night sky. "*Dishkuh.*" At least I could still swear in Djinni.

Still, swearing didn't solve my problem. Without a hunter I was back to square one. That meant it was down to me to find out the truth.

I squared my shoulders. So be it. I'd solve the murder myself. I'd already gotten a good look at the crime scene and the body. Now what?

# # #

My stomach gave an unladylike growl. All this running around trying to solve a murder was making me hungry. I needed something to eat if I wanted my brain to work properly.

Common Grounds was a quirky little coffee shop just a few blocks away from Morgan's house. I glanced at my watch. It should still be open. Granted, I ran the risk of Liz finding me gone and freaking out, but then I was a teenager. Technically. Teenagers did things like go out for coffee in the middle of the night, right?

I'd just leave out the part about the dead body.

After locking my bike up outside the shop, I hurried in to place my order. The girl behind the counter was bobbing her head to the music, her super short blond hair glimmering gold and silver in the overhead lights. She had colorful tattoos running up and down her arms and silver hoops through her ears, eyebrows, and lower lip. Pretty conservative for Portland, from what I'd seen.

Coffee in hand, I sank down on one of the couches scattered around the shop, legs tucked under me. The rich scent of roasted coffee beans tickled my nose and made my mouth water. I took a sip, swirling the sweet, creamy stuff over my tongue. My brain immediately felt marginally less befuddled. I took a large bite of the accompanying scone, my stomach gurgling happily. Okay, time to think.

Maybe someone killed Tim Newlund with a knife and then tried to cover it up by puncturing his neck to look like a vampire bite. Except that was hard to fathom. Ninety-nine percent of the population didn't even know vampires were real so nobody would buy the fact Tim had been attacked by one of the creatures. Besides, I was pretty sure the puncture marks had been made before Tim's neck had been sliced open. What kind of nitwit would sit still and let someone puncture his neck? It hadn't looked like there'd been much of struggle other than the blood on his face which hadn't appeared to have come from obvious injuries. He could have been knocked out, of course. But again, no bumps on the head. Poison, maybe? Drugs? I hadn't smelled anything, but then I was human now.

Vampire was the next logical step. For me, anyway. They'd bite first for sure. But every vampire I'd ever heard of, and I'd heard of quite a few in my time, was a crazy feral who wouldn't bother covering his, or her, crime. Vampires did not care if humans found their kills. They cared about nothing but the blood.

Unless Tim's murder was about more than food. Still, I couldn't wrap my head around vampires being able to control themselves long enough to pull off what I'd seen.

Maybe some other supernatural creature? Or some whack job who only thought he was a vampire? But then why bother slicing Tim's throat? Why not just leave him? Or break his neck? Why go to the trouble and mess?

"Well, now. Isn't this a pretty picture?" The slightly husky voice sent unexpected shivers up my spine. "A penny for your thoughts."

CHAPTER FIVE

I eyeballed the boy standing in front of me. *Young man*, I reminded myself. He might look young, but our bodies were no doubt around the same age. He looked wonderfully disreputable with his shaggy blond hair and sprayed-on denim. I took an instant liking to him. He even wore a perfectly scuffed black biker jacket and matching boots. From his chiseled cheek bones to his luscious lips he was almost too beautiful to be real. Like that Calvin person's models. Until I got a look at his eyes.

Those pretty gray-blue eyes were ancient.

"Hello, Abbie."

"Do I know you?" He did look familiar, but I couldn't place him. I wasn't about to let on that he made my blood sing. Especially when part of me was quietly freaking out. I'd never been attracted to a human before.

"Mick." He sank down on the couch next to me without asking. "We go to school together."

"Oh."

"We're both seniors. Both in AP English."

Ah, yes. I remembered him now. Or rather, Abbie remembered him. A memory surged to the forefront. He was the quiet one, always at the back of the class oozing boredom and cool. He'd arrived at the school shortly before I had taken over Abbie's body. I'd honestly never paid attention to him. How had I not noticed? So, I played dumb.

"But how do you know my name?" Her name. Not mine.

"You're Abbie Roberts. Principal's niece. Everyone knows you."

"Oh, right." I tried desperately to ignore the fact that my heart rate had picked up alarmingly. Instead I tilted my chin up and squared my shoulders. "What are you doing here?" I almost flinched at the snooty tone coming out of my mouth. I hadn't meant to sound that way, but I found myself oddly nervous.

He eyed me, those beautiful ancient eyes of his inscrutable. "I followed you."

"Excuse me?" This time the outrage was all mine.

A slight flush stained those excellent cheekbones. "I mean, I was outside and saw you come in." He shrugged as if it were perfectly normal to follow young women into coffee shops.

"Do you always follow strangers into coffee shops?" I blurted before I could stop. That was the curse of Zip. Always saying exactly what came into my head.

Was that amusement flitting across Mick's face?

"But you're not a stranger."

I sighed and took another bite of scone. "Fine. So we're not entirely strangers. Was there something you wanted?"

"Nothing in particular. I just thought it would be nice to sit down and talk. Get to know each other." Mick settled back into the leather sofa, never taking his eyes off my face. The intensity in his eyes made me squirm in ways that I hadn't since the first day I stepped into the marid's office. The corners of his mouth quirked up for a split second as if he knew what I was thinking. A tiny flicker of amusement before returning to his usual blasé expression.

I took a giant gulp of coffee, nearly scalding myself in the process. Why did he want to talk to me? We'd never talked before that I could remember.

"What did you want to talk about?" I was practically crossing my fingers hoping he didn't realize the effect he was having on me.

"Anything. Everything." His smile told me he knew exactly the effect he had on me. The big jerk.

"Listen. I'm kind of busy," I said, deliberately ignoring his long, lean legs stretched out next to me on the couch. "Maybe we can talk some other time." Like, this side of never. I did not need complications in my life. I needed a way back to the djinn.

"So, tell me, Abbie," he said, ignoring my dismissal. "What are you doing here all by yourself in the middle of the night? Shouldn't you be at home?"

I glared at him. What I did with my time was my business. No one else's.

"If you must know," I said archly, taking another sip of coffee, "I wanted to get out and have some time to myself. To think." I gave him a look. "Alone."

"And what deep thoughts have furrowed your lovely brow?"

Gods, what was his problem? Why couldn't he leave me alone? Stop staring at me with those beautiful eyes and talking to me with that sexy voice?

"Um, sorry, what?"

His smile said he knew exactly what I'd been thinking. Which was impossible. He couldn't read my mind. Could he? I mean, he looked human enough, but with my djinn abilities gone, I had no way of knowing.

He leaned in closer, the rich woodsy scent of him playing with my senses. "What is it that has you worried, lovely Abbie?"

"Nothing much," I blurted. "Just murder."

# # #

Mick Egan eyed the pretty little blonde curled up on the couch next to him, sipping delicately at a cup of coffee. To say she did strange things to his insides was an understatement. Her beauty was breathtaking. But it was more than that. She wasn't just a pretty face.

Ever since the day he'd joined the senior class he'd definitely noticed her. She was fierce and funny and smart. She spoke her mind and didn't care what anyone thought. He liked that about her.

He spent way too much time thinking about her, but he'd never quite had the courage to approach her. Until tonight.

Leaning back in his chair, he stretched out his legs, crossing them at the ankles. She watched his every move, face a mask of indifference, but her eyes were bright and he was pretty sure she was blushing. Just a little. Maybe, just maybe, she'd thought about him, too.

"So, murder is it? Who got themselves offed?" He went for cool and casual. Yeah, that was the way to go.

She shrugged. "A boy at school. Tim Newlund." Her eyes narrowed. "Did you know him? You didn't have anything to do with it, did you?"

Her accusation startled him, but he managed to keep his face straight. He'd done a lot of crap in his short life, but murder wasn't part of it. "Doubtful. I don't know any Tim Newlund so it's not likely I'd have a reason to kill him. How did he die?" He wasn't sure he really wanted to know how the kid had died, but he wanted to keep her talking to him.

"Somebody bit him, then slit his throat."

"Bit him?" That made Mick raise his eyebrow. "Like a fetish, or something?"

"More like a vampire, or something." Abbie eyed him as if she expected him to burst out laughing, but he managed not to react. Barely.

"A vampire. You know they're not real, right? You're not one of those crazy chicks that wants to date dead guys, are you?"

That got a rise out of her. "Don't be such a jerk," she snapped, slamming her mug down on the side table, scattering scone crumbs everywhere.

"Well then, be serious."

She stood, hands in fists at her sides. "I am serious. They're real, you know. Whether you believe it or not."

Damn, she was hot when she got all worked up like that. Still, he didn't want her pissed off at him.

35

Besides, what if she really did believe there were vampires? That was probably something he should figure out before he gave away too much. Otherwise she'd really think he was crazy.

"Okay, suppose that's true," he offered with a false casualness. "Why would this mysterious vampire slice open Newlund's throat after biting him? Some kind of weird ritual thing?"

"Yes, sure, why not? I mean who knows what kind of supernatural hinkyness we've got going on here?" Abbie said, zipping up her jacket as she headed for the door.

Mick stepped ahead of her to hold open the door. Maybe he'd get points for being a gentleman.

He watched her walk past, hips gently swaying in her skin-tight jeans. The sight made his own jeans uncomfortably snug.

"What are you staring at?" she snapped, jolting him out of his reverie. She bent over to unchain her bike.

"Nothing. You were saying?" he prodded.

"Right. Yes," she said, giving him a look rife with suspicion. "Okay, so maybe the vampire was pissed off about something Tim did to him, and that explains the whole knife thing." There was an edge of doubt to her voice.

"You don't believe that."

She sighed. "You're right. It doesn't make any sense. Vampires are completely feral. They wouldn't just bite some random kid in a library then slice his throat. It's stupid. I know there's got to be more to it than that."

"What do you really think?" he asked her gently, curious to hear what she'd come up with.

She started down the street, pushing her bike. She kept nibbling on her lower lip which made Mick think about kissing her. He gave himself a mental punch in the jaw.

"I think that whoever killed Tim Newlund targeted him for a reason. And that if we don't find out what that reason is and stop the killer, this city is going to be in big trouble because whatever creature did it, it's dangerous."

"'We?'" he asked, amusement and hope suddenly taking root. "Are you asking me to help you solve a murder, Abbie?"

CHAPTER SIX

"No thanks," I snapped, suddenly realizing I'd let my guard down. No way could I let this...human get involved. If there really was a supernatural creature involved, it could be dangerous. Not to mention the risk of exposing reality to his poor human brain. What would he do if he suddenly discovered everything he thought he knew was a lie? Still, part of me couldn't help but wish I had someone to confide in. Someone to lean on. I gripped the handles of my bike so tightly my knuckles turned white.

"I don't need your help. This isn't my first disco."

"Rodeo."

"What?"

"The phrase is: 'This isn't my first rodeo,'" Mick said, shoving his hands into the pockets of his jeans.

"Right. Whatever." Like I cared what the phrase was. Humans had so many it was hard to keep straight. "The point is, I can do this on my own."

The smile that crept across his face made me shiver. In a good way. "I'm happy to help," he said in that husky voice of his. The one that suddenly had me thinking naughty thoughts. "All you have to do is ask."

I opened my mouth to respond, but it was too late. He was gone, vanishing down the street so quickly he almost could have been a supernatural.

Shaking my head, I climbed onto my bike. I needed to get home before Liz freaked out. Somehow I'd figure out my next move. I could watch *CSI* for inspiration.

I cast a look behind me, but the street was empty. And while I was at it, I'd figure out why I suddenly had the hots for a boy I barely knew.

# # #

I woke to the aroma of freshly brewed coffee and with my face smooshed into my pillow. I sniffed. The coffee scent moved closer. I opened one eye to find a cup of the stuff inches from my face.

"Figured you could use a cup." It was Liz, already perfectly coiffed and ready for the day, but I could see the fine lines of strain. No amount of makeup could hide the dark circles under her eyes.

"Thanks." I sat up, rubbing the sleep from my eyes and subtly checking for drool before taking the cup from Liz's outstretched hand. I felt a little fuzzy in the brain, but I was still alert enough to realize how unusual this was. Liz had never brought me coffee in bed before. Not while I'd been in this body. Not before either, according to the memories I still retained from Abbie.

The serious expression on Liz's face told me she wanted to talk. Had she discovered my late night outing? Or that I'd been at the crime scene?

"Is something wrong, Aunt Liz?"

She sat down next to me on the bed, lacing her fingers in her lap. "Were you up late studying? Maybe if you're too tired, you should stay home today."

What in the name of *Infernus?* Liz was always on my backside about getting to school on time and now she wanted me to stay home? Surely they would have cleaned up the crime scene by now, or else she would have been forced to shut down the entire school. Did she know something? Suspect something?

"I wasn't up that late," I said gulping down half my coffee. I narrowed my eyes, searching Liz's face. "But you sure were. They keep you working late? Jerks." I kept my tone light and teasing, like I imagined a niece might do with her aunt.

Liz twisted her hands over and over in her lap, a clear sign of stress. Or distress, anyway. I set the coffee down on the nightstand and placed my hands over hers. Her hands stilled under mine and she looked startled, for which I couldn't blame her. Abbie and her aunt had not exactly been demonstrative.

"Aunt Liz, what's wrong?"

She let out a deep, trembling sigh. "The police called me last night."

"The police? What for?" I pretended surprise. Rather well, too, if I do say so myself.

'There...there was a murder at the school."

"Ohmigod," I ran the words together like I'd heard the kids at school do. "Who died? Murder? Ohmigod."

It was her turn to place her hands over mine, holding them as if she was afraid I might have a meltdown or something. Little did she know this wasn't my first dead body. After all, I'd watched my own body bleed to death on the high desert.

"Don't worry, Abbie," she said, squeezing my hands a little too tight. "Everything will be fine. The police will solve this and everything will be fine." It sounded more like she was trying to reassure herself.

"But who died?" I prompted her again, though I knew the answer.

"A sophomore boy named Tim Newlund." She gave me a sad look. "Did you know him?"

I pretended to think it over. "No. The name doesn't sound familiar. I don't really hang out with sophomores."

"No. No, of course not." She let go of my hands and stood up. "Listen, I still have to go into work today, but I think it would be best if you stayed home."

"Oh, come on, Aunt Liz, that's silly."

Liz's face hardened. I guess that had been the wrong thing to say. I tried again.

"I mean, won't people be suspicious if your niece doesn't show up to school the day after someone is murdered?"

She shook her head. "No one will suspect you, Abbie."

"I mean, they'll think, and rightly, that you kept me home because it isn't safe. Everyone will freak out. The school will turn into a ghost town." Okay, so I was being a little over dramatic, but I couldn't help myself. The djinn enjoyed a level of melodrama.

Liz shook her head, nervously twisting her gold bracelet around her wrist. "Very well, but if you feel at all unsafe or see anyone suspicious, come straight to my office, understood?"

I nodded. "Understood."

"And stay away from the library. It's still technically a crime scene and I'll have enough of a headache on my hands keeping everyone out of there."

"Of course." I gave her a saccharine sweet smile. *Like hell.*

CHAPTER SEVEN

The library doors were still sealed with yellow-and-black crime tape. I waited out of sight until the school rent-a-cop took a bathroom break. Then, ignoring the warning, I ducked under the tape and slipped inside the darkened room. The lights were off and the blinds on the windows partially closed. I could still smell the faint copper tang of blood and beneath it that sickly sweet smell of death that seemed to coat everything it touched.

The place where Tim Newlund had died was easy enough to find, despite the lack of light. Even if I hadn't smelled it, the dark stain marring the pale gray carpet would have given it away.

Sunlight filtered through the slats of the blinds, giving me just enough light to see. I crouched down next to the bloodstain, trying to pick up something, anything that might be a clue to Tim's murder. I wasn't sure what I hoped to find, but all I saw was the big old bloodstain. Maybe if I'd still been a djinni.

"Find anything, babe?"

I jerked my head up so fast, I almost fell over backward. I slapped my palm flat on the wall to balance. The painted concrete was cool under my skin which suddenly felt way too warm. "What are you doing here?" I hissed, irritated that I'd allowed Mick to sneak up on me. Though if I were honest, the sudden increase in my pulse rate had little to do with his sneakiness and everything to do with the snug fit of his jeans and the devil-may-care attitude he exuded. He reminded me of Jensen Ackles. I'd recently discovered I had a thing for Jensen Ackles.

Mick just smiled that lazy smile of his. The one that did funny things to my insides and made my heart start flip-flopping. Stupid traitor that it was. He looked insanely delicious in his military style jacket, Doc Martens casually crossed as he leaned against one of the shelves.

"You're not supposed to be here." I climbed to my feet. "It's a crime scene." That was stupid, seeing as how I was standing in said crime scene. Unfortunately it was the first thing to pop into my head.

"Just thought I'd see if you needed any help," he said lightly, but his eyes were dead serious. Beneath the false cheer, there was something deeper. Something that made the butterflies in my stomach start pole-dancing.

Shoving aside my idiotic reaction to his presence, I narrowed my eyes. "I told you, I can do this on my own. I'm not an idiot, you know."

He reached out and gently tucked a blonde curl behind my ear, his fingers lingering against my skin a fraction longer than necessary. "I never said you were."

Crossing my arms over my chest, I glared at him. "Then why are you here?"

"Call it curiosity." He leaned in closer. "I'm bored."

I rolled my eyes. "You are such a child." It wasn't true, of course. He was eighteen, a senior, and aged beyond his years. By what, I'd yet to discover. Still, if we wanted to compare birthdays, I'd totally win.

"Come on," he said with a teasing grin. "Humor me. What have you found out?"

I sighed. Well, if you couldn't beat him, you might as well drink the Kool-Aid. For now. "Fine. I thought I would check out the crime scene. See if there something was missed last night. Nothing much here. Just blood. A lot of it. I don't think this was a vampire." I said the last like I was joking, but I wasn't.

He raised an eyebrow. "You sure?"

I guess he was still playing along. "No. I'm not. But it doesn't make sense this was a vampire. If Tim was out on the street and got attacked, maybe." I glanced back at the stain. "But it was here in the library where the only people who would find him would be teachers or students."

"You think it has something to do with the school?"

"I don't know. Maybe." I uncrossed my arms and headed back across the library toward the main doors. "There's nothing here. I need to find out more about Tim Newlund. And you," I said, spinning around and pinning Mick with my best, bossy glare, "need to get out of here before someone sees you. Go to class or whatever it is you do."

"Whatever you say, babe."

I rolled my eyes as I peered out into the hallway. The guard was still gone. I turned around and shot Mick a look. "And, Mick?"

"Yeah?"

"Don't call me babe."

Mick just flashed me a cheeky grin. "Do you prefer hon?"

With a growl, I whirled around and strode down the hall, ignoring his lingering stare. But I felt it all the way down to my bones.

# # #

When Abbie was alive, she had never talked to sophomores if she could help it. From her memories, I knew that there was a certain hierarchy, and seniors were on the top of the food chain. Not that I cared about such lame things anymore, but Abbie had, once upon a time. It was important for me to keep up appearances in order to avoid awkward questions.

Unfortunately, today was a day for awkward questions. I needed to find some sophomores to talk to.

As I headed into the girls' bathroom, I kept my ears open for any chatter about Tim's murder. A couple of girls were planted in front of the mirrors applying thick coats of lip gloss. It smelled like cherries and vanilla.

"I just can't believe it," the brunette was saying. She was a slender thing, pale and a little mousy. I could teach her a thing or two about styling it up.

"I'm not surprised." The redhead shrugged, tucking away her lip gloss and producing a tube of mascara. Pulling out the wand, she began applying a fresh layer to her already overburdened lashes. "He was such a weirdo. Bet he was into all kinds of freaky stuff."

"Don't be mean. He was just shy, that's all." The brunette's voice was quiet, but she stood her ground. "We shouldn't say bad things about dead people."

"Give me a break." The redhead eyed the other girl. "Maybe you like freaks, huh?" She let out a braying laugh that made both the brunette and me flinch.

The brunette didn't say anything, but her cheeks turned bright red and she lowered her eyes. The redhead smirked and fluffed her hair. "Whatever. I gotta get to class. See you later."

I waited until the girl had sashayed out of the bathroom before joining the brunette at the mirrors. Pulling my own lip gloss out of my bag, I casually said, "Were you talking about that boy they found in the library?"

The brunette appeared a little flustered to have a senior talking to her. "Um, yeah. Tim Newlund."

"It's so sad what happened. Poor guy. You knew him?"

"A little. He was in some of my classes." The girl's cheeks were still a little pink, and she kept her eyes downcast.

"Gosh," I gushed, "must have been such a shock. Him being murdered. Who would do such a horrible thing?" I swiped a coat of gloss over my lips, eyeing the other girl in the mirror.

"I don't know." The brunette shrugged, glancing up. Her eyes were sad. "I mean he was really quiet. Everyone thought he was a little weird. Some of the guys were a bit...well, mean to him. But nobody would have killed him." She hesitated.

I just eyed her. Waiting. Sometimes you just have to play out the string and let the fish bite. What can I say? The marid had been fond of fishing. I picked up a few things.

The brunette looked around as if to make sure we were alone. Then she whispered, "If it had been suicide, I wouldn't have been surprised. I don't think anyone would have been." There was something in her tone that told me the girl understood exactly how Tim Newlund had felt. "But murder?" She shook her head, shoving her lip gloss back in her bag. "It's just strange, you know?" She gave me a wobbly smile and hurried after her friend.

I watched her go, my mind racing. A bullied boy, whose suicide wouldn't have been a surprise, had turned up murdered instead. Interesting.

I propped my hands on my hips and stared thoughtfully at my reflection. I needed to find out more about Tim Newlund.

CHAPTER EIGHT

I smoothed down the full skirt of my royal blue, fifties-style dress and ran my fingers through my hair. The black cardigan and ballet flats made the outfit pretty, but somber enough for visiting the bereaved. I double-checked to make sure the clasp on my necklace hadn't slid around to the front. Once I was sure everything was perfect, I rapped on the front door of the mid-century modern split level house. The style might be all the rage according to those house hunting shows, but this one had seen better days. The door swung open almost immediately, revealing a plain looking middle-aged woman in a navy blue pantsuit.

"Yes?"

"Mrs. Newlund?"

The woman shook her head. "No, I'm Maggie's sister, Jean." The fine lines around the woman's mouth and eyes deepened.

"I'm Zi-" I caught myself. No one in my new life called me Zip. "I'm Abbie Roberts." I gave Jean a smile that I hoped imparted both sympathy and friendliness. "Principal Roberts' niece. I came to give Mrs. Newlund my condolences. And," I lifted a baking dish covered in aluminum foil, "I made her a casserole."

It wasn't necessarily my favorite way to spend a Saturday morning, but it was what people did according to some of the articles I'd read online. Having never baked a casserole I was somewhat dubious about the results, but palatability wasn't my main concern. This was all about camouflage.

"How thoughtful of you. Won't you come in, dear?" Jean stepped back, waving me into the house. "I'm sure Maggie would like to see one of Tim's friends. She's right through there."

"Thank you." I didn't bother to correct Jean's assumption that Tim and I had been friends. She took the casserole and nodded in the direction of what was clearly the living room. "I don't suppose I could use your bathroom first?"

Jean looked mildly surprised. "Of course. Just up the stairs to your right." With that she disappeared into the kitchen.

The stairs were narrow and covered in a well-worn, dusty pink carpet that had been out of style for at least twenty years. The stairway itself was lined with faux wood paneling and hung with photographs of Tim at every stage of his life. It was actually kind of sad.

Each step creaked and shifted under my feet as I made my way up. Fortunately the hall floor wasn't nearly as bad. I found the bathroom immediately. Glancing around to make sure I was alone, I continued on down the narrow hallway, feet silent on the teal carpet that was as badly worn as the pink.

I opened each door along the hallway until I came to a room that was clearly Tim's. Slipping in, I shut the door carefully behind me and glanced around. The place was a disaster.

Piles of clothes, mostly dirty if the smell was anything to go by, littered the floor. Geeky sci-fi posters plastered the walls to the point where you couldn't even see the paint. There were stacks of comic books everywhere and shelves jammed with action figures coated in dust, some of them still in their boxes. Pushed up against the window was a desk piled with sketches signed by Tim Newlund. I picked one up, my eyes widening in surprise and disgust.

"Ew."

I quickly put it back down. The image was graphic and violent. I was no stranger to violence, but the picture turned my stomach. Apparently Tim had found at least one way to vent his rage against the bullies at school. He had also been a halfway decent artist, despite his choice of material.

Oddly there was no computer, no TV, no gaming station. I didn't even see an iPad or anything. Which was really strange for a teenage geek like Tim. Maybe they were just too poor? Or maybe his parents were those crazy anti-technology types. As far as I could tell, he hadn't kept a journal, either. Just dozens of drawings of him exacting his revenge on his tormentors.

My ears suddenly picked up what sounded like my name. Or rather, Abbie's name. The voices were easily heard through the thin walls of the old house. Tuning in to the conversation below, I heard Jean say, "She must be up in the bathroom still. Maybe I'd better check on her."

Moving as fast as I could, I was out of Tim's room, down the hall, and in the bathroom before Jean was halfway up the stairs. Quickly I flushed the toilet and then ran the water in the sink for a few seconds, emerging just as Jean arrived outside the door.

"Are you all right, Miss Roberts?"

"I'm sorry. I think I ate something bad for lunch." I clutched at my stomach and hunched my shoulders as though I was about to be sick. "I probably should go home. Can you please give my apologies to Mrs. Newlund and tell her I'm really sorry about Tim?"

"But of course." Jean tutted in sympathy, patting me on the back. "Take care of yourself. Get some rest and drink lots of fluids."

With a nod I headed down the stairs and out the door as fast as I could without looking suspicious. At least I knew for sure that Tim had been bullied. Where that left me, I had no idea.

# # #

"Visiting the bereaved. How charitable of you." The lazy voice startled me out of my thoughts.

"Mick." I glared at the young man lounging in the rocker on my front porch. Every long, lean inch of him. He looked totally at home. The sunlight glinted golden on his hair and the intensity in his eyes turned my legs to jelly. "Have you been spying on me again?"

"Not spying, babe." His blue eyes sparkled and his full, kissable lips quirked up in a smile.

Kissable lips? Oh, good grief. I had to stop thinking things like that. He was...human. Okay, so was I, but he was far too young for me. "Stalking, then."

That made him smile even wider. "Would I stalk you?"

"Yes," I snapped.

He laid a hand over his heart. "Why do you wound me so, dearest Abbie?"

I rolled my eyes and stomped up the porch steps. "Get over it."

I quickly unlocked the door, hoping to slip in and shut it in his face. No such luck. He was stronger and faster than I'd given him credit for. Before I could blink, he'd grabbed the door and slipped inside before I could close it. The entry way suddenly felt a little too small for the two of us.

"Why are you here, Mick?" I turned around to hang my jacket in the hall closet. I never kept my coats downstairs, but I needed to do something to keep my hands busy and my eyes off of Mick. I turned around to find him inches away.

"Because, sweet Abbie," he said, leaning in until his face was within kissing distance of mine, "you need my help whether you admit it or not."

"No, I don't," I said, dropping my keys into my handbag and ignoring the sudden desire to lean into him. "I'm doing fine on my own." I moved past him into the kitchen. Dropping my purse on the table, I opened the refrigerator and rummaged around, pulling out a bottle of mango juice.

"What have you found out so far?" he asked, one eyebrow raised. "Let me guess. Tim Newlund had no friends, was a total geek, and was bullied by half the school. How am I doing so far?"

"That's about it," I admitted reluctantly, pouring myself a glass of juice. "How did you find out?"

"I have my sources." His grin was pure wickedness. It did funny things to my insides.

"Well, maybe your sources should focus on finding out something useful," I said, my voice a little more breathless than I wanted. It was one thing to play simpering maiden. It was another thing to actually be one. I stiffened my spine and rolled back my shoulders.

Suddenly Mick was right there in my space, face inches from mine. My heart rate sped up and I felt my cheeks warming. I had to make myself set down the glass before I ended up spilling my drink all over myself.

"And what would I get out of it?" His voice was low and husky and sent shivers down my spine.

"What do you mean?"

His blue eyes practically smoldered. "If I help you, what do I get out of it? Another date, perhaps?"

"Hey, I didn't ask you here. You're the one that keeps showing up wanting to help." I had to get control of things before I did something really stupid. Like kiss him. "Besides, we haven't even been on a first date yet."

"What do you call the coffee shop then?"

"That was not a date."

"Well, let's just say you owe me one, then." His mouth was a breath away from mine. My brain went totally fuzzy. All I could do was stare at his lips, wishing...

My cell phone rang, jarring me out of whatever trance Mick had put me in. Saved by the bell.

Backing away from him I pulled out my phone. "Hello?"

It was Aunt Liz. "Abbie, thank God. Where are you?"

"Hi, Aunt Liz. I'm at home. Why?"

She sighed. "No reason, I just wanted to make sure." Her voice sounded a little strangled. Like maybe she'd been crying.

"What's wrong, Aunt Liz?" I wanted to demand that she tell the truth, not to lie, but that was more likely to get her back up than sounding sympathetic and worried.

"Nothing. Everything...just...you need to stay away from the school, okay?"

"What? Why?" I had a really bad feeling.

Mick reached out and laid his hand over mine. The contact sent sparks dancing along my nerve endings, but I also felt safe.

Liz paused. Then she finally blurted out, "There's been another accident, Abbie."

Accident, my ass. But I played it to the hilt. "Oh my god, who? Where?"

55

"I'll talk to you about it when I get home tonight, okay? In the meantime, just stay inside with the doors locked, all right? Promise me, Abbie."

After making promises I had no intention of keeping, I finally hung up. I remembered just in time to swear in English. "Crap."

Concern flashed across Mick' face, quickly replaced by his usual blend of laid-back cockiness. "Something wrong, babe?"

"There's been another murder."

CHAPTER NINE

The second body was sprawled in the middle of the gym floor, eyes wide, limbs splayed out at odd angles. Just like Tim, the girl's throat had been slashed from ear to ear. A bright pink backpack lay next to her in a pool of congealed blood.

"Oh no," I whispered.

I recognized her immediately: the brunette girl from the bathroom. The one who'd told me about Tim being bullied. The one whose "friend" had been so mean and nasty. I felt physically ill. Mick moved closer, almost as if he could feel how upset I was. I found his presence surprisingly comforting.

We crouched beneath the bleachers, the dark shadows hiding us from the uniforms milling around. It had been easy enough to slip in behind the coroner's assistants as they wheeled in a gurney to collect the body.

Liz was standing a few feet from the body, dabbing her eyes with a white handkerchief. Not a Kleenex, but a proper square of cloth like they did in the old days. Monogrammed and everything. Beside her stood the same detective who'd been at Tim's crime scene. I recognized his voice.

"She was killed sometime last night. The janitor found her body this morning and called us in. You recognize her?"

"Yes, of course." Liz straightened her shoulders and tucked away her hankie. She was now in full principal mode. "Dana Smith. She was a sophomore. Intelligent, but fairly quiet. Not very popular, but friends with some of the more popular students." Liz shook her head. "Poor kid. She didn't deserve this...this horrible thing."

"I talked to her the other day at school," I said, keeping my voice pitched so only Mick could hear me. A feeling of sadness and regret welled up inside. "I didn't even get her name."

Guilty. That was it. I felt guilty. Which was ridiculous. This wasn't my fault. But it made me more determined to stop whoever was killing these kids.

"Was she in any way connected to the previous victim?" The detective glanced over at the coroner who crouched next to Dana's body, carefully avoiding the pool of blood.

"I don't believe so, they weren't friends as far as I know," Liz said, studiously avoiding looking at Dana's body. "But they had some classes together. It's possible they knew each other."

"She said he was bullied." I whispered to Mick. I wondered if Dana had been bullied, too. The redhead girl she'd been with certainly hadn't been very nice to her.

"You think that's true?" Mick asked.

"Yeah. It's definitely true."

"Do we have a serial killer on our hands?" Liz's voice was stronger now. As if she were trying to reassert control.

"Ma'am, I'm sorry, but I can't discuss that with you..."

"I'm not an idiot, Detective." Liz turned her full Glare of Death on the man. "I have eyes. Her throat was slashed. Just like Tim Newlund's."

I didn't wait to hear the detective's answer. I knew what it would be. "Come on. Let's get out of here. I've seen enough."

Mick nodded and reached out to grab my hand. Those stupid sparks zinged again as skin touched skin. I followed him under the bleachers and around to the other side of the gym where we slipped through the door to the boys' locker room. Either the cops didn't think it worth guarding or someone was shirking their duty, but we managed to make our way out of the locker room and eventually out of the school without being seen.

Once we were outside, Mick turned to me. "What do you think?" He kept his voice low.

"I think somebody, or something, slashed her throat. And I bet that, just like Tim, there are bite marks under the cut." I still wasn't convinced it was an actual vampire going around biting people. Unfortunately, I had no idea what else it could be. There wasn't a lot to go on.

"What do you think it means?"

I glanced over at Mick who was clearly still humoring me. "No idea. How about you? Any ideas?"

Mick gave me a sly look. The one that told me he was plotting something. "Maybe. I'll let you know."

# # #

"Okay, spill," I said the minute we were far enough away from the school we wouldn't be heard. I was not exactly good with the whole patience-as-a-virtue thing.

"Spill what, babe?" His tone, one of innocence, didn't fool me a bit.

I stopped right in front of him, arms crossed over my chest. "I'm not moving until you tell me what you're up to. And don't call me babe. I know girls think it's cute, but women find it condescending."

He was silent for a minute. "I'm sorry. I didn't mean it that way."

I sighed. "I know. Call me Zip." I turned around and started walking again, oddly nervous.

"Why Zip?" He kept pace beside me, our arms almost touching.

"It's...what those who are close to me call me."

His eyes got all warm at that which made me squirm a little. "Okay, Zip. I'm sorry."

I decided to give him some grace. "You said you wanted to help. Now, help."

"I said I'd help, but you'll owe me." The wicked, teasing smile was back.

"Fine. I owe you." I didn't know what game he was playing at, but I was feeling reckless. I also decided to ignore the feeling of excitement that surged at the thought of spending more time with him. Seriously, I needed to get my head examined. "Now what do you know?"

"Nothing more than you, Zip."

"But you have some ideas. You have a plan. I know you do." I'd seen it in his eyes.

"Ideas, some. A plan, definitely."

"Ugh, you are annoying."

Mick just smirked. Then his tone turned serious. "Will you be at home tonight?"

I was completely baffled by both the question and his sudden change of mood. "Yeah, why?"

"Good." He gave me an innocent look. I didn't buy it for a minute. "I'll pick you up at dusk."

I raised an eyebrow. "Excuse me?"

"You want to find out who the killer is, don't you?"

"Yes, of course." What was he getting at?

"Well, then, babe. I think it's time for a stakeout. Wear something sexy."

And with that he was gone, leaving me gaping after him. "What the..." I shook my head. "Sexy my backside."

What I needed was less Mick and more chocolate.

I ignored the little voice that told me that chocolate would never be nearly as satisfying as a certain mysterious young man.

CHAPTER TEN

I slipped silently through the halls of the high school, trying desperately to keep my attention focused on anything but the man at my side. Mick had a way of getting under my skin. Worse, I was starting to like it.

"You call that sexy?" His voice was a whisper, but I heard him just fine.

Shooting him a scowl I said, "I wasn't going for sexy. I was going for practical. And there's nothing wrong with what I'm wearing." My simple jeans, sweater, and boots made a lot more sense than whatever Mick was imagining. I'd bet a week's supply of donuts on it. Besides, he was sexy enough for both of us in his tight black t-shirt and jeans ensemble. "Why are we here, anyway?"

"Come on, Zip." He didn't say it exactly, but his tone told me he expected more from me.

I sighed. He was right. I could do better. I'd just been too focused on the sparks zinging through my system. "Fine. Both murders happened here at the school and both victims were students."

"So, if there's another murder..." Mick prompted, his lips twitching slightly in what was no doubt amusement at my expense.

I nearly growled at him. "It'll probably be another student here at the school." And if prior murders were anything to go by, it would no doubt be someone who was bullied. I paused to peer around a corner into the cafeteria. All clear. "Aren't we supposed to be stopping the murderer?"

"That's the plan."

"I don't know why you insisted on helping," I said as I started across the cafeteria, weaving my way around the cheap plastic tables and chairs. "I'm perfectly capable of doing this myself." I really didn't want him getting hurt. I kept forgetting I was as fragile as he was now.

He was quiet for a minute. "Of course you are."

"Then why? Why get involved at all?"

The look he shot me spoke volumes. "You know why."

I shivered, my whole body totally aware of him. How did he do this to me? How was it that he was so very different from the other guys his age? Why was it that I was starting not to care about the ten millennia age difference?

I stopped in the middle of the dark room. "Listen, Mick..."

"Shhhh," he hissed, grabbing my arm, every line of his body suddenly on alert.

I frowned, listening for whatever it was he could hear. Nothing. I opened my mouth to say so when, suddenly, the ceiling erupted in a shower of broken acoustic tiles. Something crashed to the floor a couple feet in front of us, sending chairs skittering across the room. Then the thing launched itself straight at Mick.

It hit him so hard, Mick went flying across the room and crashed into the cafeteria wall. I didn't even have time to react as, with a blood chilling snarl, the creature turned and tackled me. We went down in a heap with me at the bottom. Using our momentum, I managed to roll to the side and shove the creature off me before scrambling to my feet. My victory only lasted a moment.

The creature sprang, hitting me full in the chest. I flew backwards, head smacking the tile floor so hard my vision went dark for a split second. Pain shot up my spine and lodged itself inside my skull. It was so intense I nearly threw up, but there was no time.

The creature went for my throat, snarling and snapping, fangs bared. I caught the image of wild, matted hair and rows of razor sharp teeth. Fetid breath made me gag, bile rising again. I fought it back.

Grabbing the thing around the throat with what little strength I had left, it suddenly registered that it wasn't a creature, exactly. It was a person. Or rather, it was half a person. It was also half demon, and unfortunately at the moment, it was completely crazed and stronger than I was.

But Zip Roberts was no wimp, for all that I was human now. With every ounce of my strength, I held the demon off, trying to get the right leverage. If only I had djinn strength, I could snap its neck. As it was, I'd have to do the best I could.

The demon lunged for me again. I managed to push its head aside, so its teeth sank into my shoulder instead of my throat. The pain was excruciating. I couldn't help the scream that tore from my throat.

Then suddenly the demon was gone, flying across the room. It crashed into a table before falling to the floor, glazed eyes locked on its attacker.

Mick stood over it like an avenging angel. A really bad one. His eyes were hard and angry. He clutched a broken chair leg in one fist. I felt a tiny thrill of fear laced with excitement. He'd protected me. Risked his life for me. No one but Morgan had ever done that. Not even the marid.

Mick stalked toward the demon. Reaching down, he grabbed it and yanked it up off the floor. He lifted the makeshift club in his hand as if to strike.

"Mick, no!"

Mick hesitated, glancing back at me, chest heaving. He was still in full on rage mode, but he was waiting. For me.

Pushing myself up off the floor, I staggered toward him, one hand pressed to the back of my head. If felt a throb of pain at every step. "If you kill it, we'll never get the answers we need."

"Answers? What answers? We just need to stop the killing." He glanced from me to the demon and back again. He seemed totally unsurprised to be facing down an actual monster.

"We've got to know why it's here. We've got to know if there's more of them." I didn't mention that being half demon, the creature was also half human. I couldn't just let it be killed.

Finally with a sigh, some of the anger retreated from his face. "The things I do for you, babe."

"I told you," I panted, "not to call me babe."

He grinned, anything but contrite. "Sorry. Zip."

I took another step toward them when the world suddenly took a sharp dip to the left before spinning wildly round and round. I felt myself crash to the floor, the cold tile rushing up to meet my cheekbone. I didn't even feel the pain.

"Zip!"

Through a fog I saw the demon, no longer the focus of Mick's attention, wrap its hands around one of the cafeteria chairs. I tried to say something, to warn him, but my mouth wouldn't cooperate. Instead I watched in horror as the demon, wielding the chair like a weapon, smacked Mick across the shoulders. As Mick staggered under the attack, the demon took off in a blur.

The blur expanded, taking over my entire field of vision. And finally, it went blissfully dark.

# # #

The world came back slowly, trickling into my consciousness a little at a time. The sound of a car driving by. Animals rustling outside in the bushes. The feel of somebody sitting beside me, stroking my hair.

I opened my eyes a fraction, hissing as bright light hit my retinas. The light immediately shut off, plunging the room into near darkness. At least I knew I was in my own room, but I had no idea how I'd gotten there. The last thing I knew I was at the school.

"Sorry, sweetheart. Is that better?" The hand stroked my forehead ever so gently.

My heart gave the oddest little flutter at the tenderness in his voice. He'd called me sweetheart. Nobody had ever called me that.

I opened my eyes again. This time the only light came from the streetlight outside. "Much." My voice was a little croaky. "What happened?"

"I saved your life." No false modesty. No superiority. He didn't even smirk. Just a statement of fact.

I mulled that over. "Thanks. I guess that's two I owe you."

He smiled at that. "You better believe it."

"How'd I get here?"

"I carried you."

Hot damn, that was a long way to carry someone. He must be stronger than he looked. "It was bad, wasn't it?"

"Yes." From the look on his face it had been a lot more than bad. Apparently I'd hit the floor harder than I thought. Good thing I was immortal. At least on the inside.

I touched my shoulder. It was tender where the demon had ripped it open, but scar tissue had already formed. Djinn energy to the rescue. Other than a little bit of a boost with my senses, healing was apparently all it was good for. Thank gods Aunt Liz was working at her second job. She'd have freaked if she'd seen me. I guess I could thank the Portland school system for paying their teachers crap.

"The demon?"

"Is that what it was?" His face was impassive. I couldn't tell if he was freaking out or what. He'd gone from knowing nothing about the world around us to being attacked by a demon. How could he be so calm?

"Actually, I think it was a half-demon. It was clearly at least part human."

"That can happen?"

I shrugged. "It's rare, but yes. Where is it?"

He shook his head. "Gone. But don't worry. I'll track her down."

Her. The demon had been a girl. Unfortunately I hadn't gotten a good enough look at her to see who it was. I reached out and grabbed Mick's hand. "Don't kill her. We need to question her. Promise me."

His face was so still I couldn't even begin to guess what he was thinking. "Mick?"

"Shhhh." He squeezed my hand before letting go. "You need to rest, Zip."

"You must have questions." How could he not?

"Later. I've got a meeting and you need sleep."

I gave a slight nod. He was right. The djinn energy had healed the worst of the damage, but not all of it. I still had one hell of a headache.

He gently tucked the duvet around me, smoothing out the wrinkles as if that would help me sleep better. Then before I could so much as blink, he'd bent down and brushed his lips over mine. Feather soft and whisper sweet. Then he was gone.

CHAPTER ELEVEN

He didn't like leaving her alone. Which was ridiculous. He barely knew her. Besides, she was strong, tough. She'd be fine.

Still, all Mick wanted to do was turn around, take the stairs to Zip's room two at a time, and sit there until she woke up. He was a moron. Who was standing in the middle of her front porch with an idiotic grin on his face.

He scrubbed his hand over his face. Lord, he needed a meeting. Now.

An hour later he was feeling himself again and the urge had passed. Sharing always helped, although he left out the part about demons. Two murders was enough without the bizarre details. They wouldn't believe him anyway. Worse, they'd think he was using again.

He also left out his sudden attraction to a strange girl named Abbie. Or Zip. Or whatever. There was a mystery there and he was bound and determined to solve it. But it was his alone.

For instance, how did she know about demons and vampires? One look and she'd known their attacker was a half-demon. Not exactly common knowledge. He was certain she wasn't a hunter. So, what was she? And what had happened to turn her from a boring, ordinary girl he'd barely noticed, to a woman full of zest and energy? One he couldn't stop thinking about. Yep, she was a mystery all right. And not the only one.

He needed to track down that demon before she killed someone else. Fortunately, he had one small clue. Giving himself a mental shake, Mick headed toward the high school.

While he'd been struggling with the demon, he'd caught the smell of something. Underneath the scent of blood and dust and unwashed demon, there'd been an odd metallic tang. Not the sweet copper of blood, but the rusty iron of old pipes. And something else. Something greasy and gritty. Some kind of oil. Something mechanical.

The school building was almost one hundred years old. Lots of places for a demon to hide out and avoid being seen. Not so many of them that smelled like that.

The school was closed up tight for the weekend and classes on Monday had been cancelled thanks to frightened parents yanking their kids out of school. That left the building free for him to explore.

Slipping into the school, Mick took the first set of stairs he found that led down. Unfortunately they led only to a brightly lit and extremely clean storage room. He could find no other way in or out other than an emergency exit leading to a side yard and a couple of small windows high up on the wall. Not exactly the place a half-demon would hang out. Too open. Too exposed.

He took the stairs back to the ground floor and headed further down the hall. He was still pretty new to the school, but he remembered there was another set of stairs not far away.

The second stairway was more promising. It dead-ended at a locked fire door. Fortunately, the lock was no match for his special skill set. When you were out on your own from the age of fourteen, you developed heightened senses, found ways to survive. Including breaking and entering. A few minutes with his tools and the door swung open.

Mick pulled a flashlight out of the pocket of his black leather jacket and turned it on. The beam revealed a short, dark hallway with a door on either side and one directly ahead. The side doors were unlocked. Nothing but storage closets for the janitor.

The third door, however, was stenciled with faded orange letters: DANGER. He smiled. No teenager could resist that.

Pushing open the door he shined the flashlight around. He found himself standing on a narrow metal platform with half a dozen metal steps leading down into a large, windowless room. A hulking metal object squatted in the corner, silent and brooding. The old unused boiler room that had since been replaced by a more modern heating system. A perfect place for a demon to hide.

He sniffed the air. And by the smell of it, he'd hit the jackpot. He recognized the oily, mechanical smell along with the strong reek of BO.

Careful to make no sound, he descended the steps to the concrete floor. Playing the light over every corner, he caught a flash of silver half hidden by the bulk of the boiler. Stepping closer he saw it was the zipper on an old sleeping bag.

Along with the bag were a couple dingy pillows, a half empty water bottle, several empty chip bags and candy wrappers, and a pile of blood stained towels. No doubt the demon had used them in an attempt to clean up after the murders. This was definitely the place. But where was the demon?

# # #

"You searched the entire school?"

"Of course," Mick said with a nonchalant shrug, settling back against the cheap vinyl of the booth.

I didn't buy his casual attitude. It must have taken him half the night, while I'd been sleeping off a stupid concussion.

Taking a sip of my cola, I leaned forward, elbows on the table. The Bread & Ink was pretty empty this time of day, but I didn't want to risk anyone overhearing us.

"So, now what?" I asked, keeping my voice low.

Mick's expression didn't change, but his eyes grew somehow more intense. More heated. I felt myself blushing for no reason. I really needed to snap out of it. "What? What are you looking at?"

"You know what I'm looking at, Zip." His voice was low, rough, and totally sexy. I was in big trouble.

"Focus, Mick," I snapped. I so could not deal with my hormones right now. Never mind his. "We need

73

to figure out how to find the demon and stop her before she does any more damage."

"And how do you suggest we do that?"

"I don't know. Track her or something."

"I tried."

I almost growled in frustration. "And?"

"And, like I said, nothing. I followed some blood smears to a side exit. Once I got outside, the trail was gone."

I frowned. "Great. We're screwed."

Mick grinned. "Not necessarily." He tossed back what was left of his coffee.

"You have a plan?"

He just shrugged. "You may not like it."

"Well, spill."

"We wait for the next body to show up."

"Are you insane?" I hissed. "That is not a plan."

His blue eyes darkened. "What do you expect, Zip? We're not hunters."

I felt the color drain from my cheeks. "How do you know about hunters?"

"I know about a lot of things." His expression gave nothing away.

"Like?"

"Why do you want me to call you Zip?"

I blinked, surprised by the subject change. "Um, it's my...nickname."

His eyes narrowed. "I've never heard anyone call you that."

I took another sip of my cola, playing nonchalant, but inside my heart was hammering like a hummingbird. I could not tell Mick the truth. How would I ever explain? I would sound like a crazy person. Knowing about hunters and demons was one thing, but the djinn? We'd stayed hidden far too well and for good reason. "You haven't known me very long."

Mick leaned back in his seat, eyeing me closely. "No. I haven't."

It stung, his refusal to trust me. But I got it. I did. I nodded.

"Maybe," his voice was low and husky and sang through my blood. "You'll trust me enough to tell me your secrets."

I swallowed as I looked into his eyes. It felt as though he was trying to see into my soul. "Maybe," I said. "And maybe one day you'll trust me with yours."

CHAPTER TWELVE

"We can't just sit around and wait for another innocent person to be murdered," I said, changing the subject. We had more important things to worry about than our secrets. I clenched my hands around the icy cold glass willing my heart rate to calm down. Human emotions were so...excitable.

"What do you propose we do?" Mick asked calmly, his eyes on the empty coffee cup he twirled back and forth between his hands.

"Find the demon and stop her, of course. Just like we said."

"And how do you propose we do that, exactly?"

"You found her lair." That sounded so melodramatic. "Or whatever you want to call it. We can wait until she comes back. Grab her again." And this time we wouldn't screw it up. I wouldn't screw it up.

Mick tilted his head so the overhead light shone off his hair, revealing highlights of red among all the gold. His eyes were impossibly blue against his navy shirt, like the color of the sky in summer. I gulped my drink, willing my brain to behave.

"Yes," he said finally. "I found her lair. She'd be a fool to return."

"You and I wouldn't return," I said. "Nor would most regular demons. But this girl isn't like us, and she isn't a regular demon."

"What is she, exactly? I've never heard of a half-demon before."

Which meant he'd heard of a full demon. Curiouser and curiouser. I so wanted to ask him how he knew about the supernatural, but we had an agreement. He'd tell when I did. And I wasn't ready to spill my guts just yet. The guileless, trusting Zip was gone forever. I'd been tainted by the human part of me. By Abbie.

"I'm no expert," I warned him, "but I do know that there are certain kinds of demons that are, under the right circumstances, compatible with humans. There are ancient records that tell of demon halflings born of human women."

"Interesting. I'd love to see those records." Mick's gaze was too intense.

I ignored his comment, swirling my straw through the remains of melted ice. "They appeared normal, human, but few survived past a year or two. Those that did changed. Sometime between puberty and their early twenties, they went insane. Ripping through entire villages. Slaughtering anything that moved."

"That's not quite our girl, or the whole school would be trashed by now."

I nodded. "She's got more control, but not enough. That's why she can't stop herself, but she feels remorse. Tries to cover it up. Maybe she hasn't fully changed yet, or maybe she's not really a halfling. Maybe she's a quarter or something. I doubt she's thinking straight. That boiler room is a safe place to her. She will go back there." I'd be willing to bet on it.

"Fine," he said. "You've convinced me. Meet you in the boiler room tonight after dark." He stood up and threw a few bills on the table. Then before I could so much as blink, he'd swooped down and kissed me full on the mouth.

Then he was gone, leaving me staring after him with my mouth open.

# # #

The boiler room was exactly as Mick had described it: dank, musty, and full of dust. I could also detect the rusty metal smell of old pipes coupled with something not unlike motor oil. Underneath all that was the very faint coppery tang of blood. I had an oddly sensitive nose for a human. It made me wonder if it was the effects of my djinn energy, or if Abbie had been something special.

I shone my flashlight around, but I couldn't tell if Mick was there yet or not. I picked my way slowly down the metal steps, trying to avoid touching the railing. It, like everything else, was covered in a layer of grime and draped with thick cobwebs. Seriously gross.

Once I reached the bottom, I carefully moved toward the old boiler where Mick had said he'd found the demon's nest. A head popped out from behind the hulking iron beast, startling me so badly, I let out a little squeak.

"Oh, my god. Don't freak me out like that."

"Well, then, stop making enough noise to wake the dead, babe." Mick gave me a bright, cheeky grin.

I scowled at him, ignoring the 'babe,' and peered behind the boiler. The hiding space was tight. A little too tight. We'd have to almost be pressed up against each other. My head told me that was a bad idea. My heart told me something else entirely.

"You expect me to hide in there with you." It wasn't a question.

Something moved in his eyes. I couldn't put a name on it, but it made me happy and sad and sort of achy at the same time. Swallowing hard, I held his gaze. I wasn't sure if I was daring him or defying him. Maybe both.

Without a word, Mick took my hand and pulled me into the tight space between the back of the boiler and the concrete wall. He wasn't a big man. Not much taller than I was and leanly muscled rather than broad, but his energy seemed to fill the entire space. I could feel the warmth of his body even through our layers of clothing. His gaze never left mine, making it hard for me to breathe. I'd never ever had this reaction to a man. Especially not to a human.

Finally I glanced down, trying to break the spell only to discover he was still holding my hand, our fingers twined together. "Um, Mick..."

"Shhhhh." He leaned forward, whispering in my ear. "We're on a stakeout, remember?"

As he pulled back, his lips brushed my cheek. Was it an accident or on purpose? Either way, I felt my whole body shiver in response.

He caught my gaze again, the expression in his eyes so intense, my brain suddenly stopped working. The air around us grew thick and heavy. I felt my breath quickening, my heart pounding faster. Was it my imagination or was his face a little closer?

Against my better judgment, I felt my body sway towards his. As if that were possible in the small space. All I wanted was for him to kiss me again. Really kiss me.

We were a breath apart, bodies touching from chest to toe. Yes, he was definitely going to kiss me.

And then the screaming started.

CHAPTER THIRTEEN

I pounded up the metal stairs, hot on Mick's heels. He threw open the fire door hard. It crashed into the wall with an ear-shattering bang. He dashed up the main staircase and through the hallways so fast, I could hardly keep up. Then he stopped so abruptly I crashed into his back.

Peering around him I gasped in shock, my blood turning ice cold. It looked like a scene from a horror movie. Way worse than either of the previous crime scenes.

The school janitor lay in the middle of the hallway. His wheelie bucket, the mop handle still sticking out, had been kicked a few feet down the hallway. Everything in between, from the fronts of the metal lockers to the crappy vinyl flooring, was splashed in thick, red blood.

Half the janitor's throat had been ripped out, exposing the white bone beneath. There was a gash across his stomach so deep, his guts were spilling out onto the floor.

The demon girl knelt over the janitor's body, a kitchen knife in one hand, long lank hair hanging in her face. Her clothes were covered in blood, old and new, and other globby bits I didn't want to think about. Blood dripped from her chin and splattered onto the body. She was mumbling something over and over as she carefully

81

slashed the knife across what was left of the victim's throat. "Got to cover it up. Got to cover it up. Can't let them see. Can't let them see."

I started forward, but Mick grabbed my arm and held me back. "There was no blood when she cut him," he whispered. "He's already dead. There's nothing we can do."

I knew that. I did. But that didn't stop me from wanting to do something, anything, to stop the horror in front of me. My stomach churned and I was half afraid I'd lose my lunch right there in the school hallway.

The demon glanced up then, her eyes glazed as she peered through the dark veil of her hair. It seemed to take her a minute to register that there were other people in the hallway with her.

"Talk to her, Zip."

I did not want to talk to a deranged killer. To a demon. The irony that one of my natural forms as a djinni had been demonic didn't escape me. "Why me?"

"Because people like you."

I shot him a glare. "You are insane." As a comeback, it was pathetic. Granted, I did have a way with people, if I really wanted to. Humans had always fascinated me from the first day I'd stepped out of djinn lands. It was time to figure out if that charm extended to half-demons who needed a trip to the loony bin.

Besides, I couldn't afford to freak out over a little demon girl. Not if I wanted to survive my experience as a human. I had too much knowledge of the real world to hide behind ignorance, like most people did.

Slowly, I stepped out from behind Mick. "Hey," I called softly. The demon honed in on me, eyes wild, knife raised.

"It's okay." I raised my hands slowly, palms out. With every fiber of my being I willed her to hear me. To understand. "I'm not here to hurt you. I just want to help."

The demon's eyes darted from me to Mick and back again. She still seemed totally out of it.

"My name's Zip." I carefully moved around to the left, trying to get the girl's eyes off Mick. "Zip Roberts. Listen, I know you didn't mean to hurt anyone."

The girl opened her mouth. Closed it. Finally she said, "I know you."

"Yeah, that's right." I kept my voice light and cheerful as if we were chatting over coffee instead of a dead body, drained of blood. "I'm a senior here." With the hair out of her face, I vaguely recognized the girl but couldn't put a name to the face. "You're a sophomore, right?"

The demon girl's mouth worked. "Sophomore, yes," she finally said as if the words were a struggle to get out.

"What's your name?" Maybe if I could get the girl to remember her human side, we could stop her from running. Or killing.

"Name." The girl looked confused for a moment. Then her expression cleared. "Zoe."

83

"Good. Listen, why don't you put the knife down so we can talk?"

Apparently that was exactly the wrong thing to say. With an angry scream, Zoe threw the knife so hard I barely had time to duck out of the way as it buried itself to the hilt in the wall behind me. Then the demon girl took off running.

# # #

"Not again," Mick growled before taking off after Zoe with me hot on his heels.

I flew through the halls as fast as my feet would carry me, but they were faster, disappearing around a corner. A door slammed up ahead. It sounded like the front door. Great, they were out on the street. Just what this city needed: a public death match between a teenager and a demon.

I rounded the corner and hit the crash bar, exiting the school and cutting across the front lawn. There. Just up ahead I could see the two of them headed across the street toward the park. Good. At least the trees would provide some cover from curious eyes.

As I hit the park, I could hear the sounds of a fight up ahead. "Fantastic," I muttered to myself. Somehow I had to stop Zoe from ripping Mick's head off. Easier said than done.

I entered the center of the park just in time to see Mick crash into a tree trunk before sliding to the ground. I started to go to him, but he jumped to his feet, brushing a strand of blond hair out of his eyes. Thank the gods he was all right. For now.

Zoe crouched a few feet away, hissing like an animal, rows of sharp teeth flashing in the moonlight. Two prominent fangs sprouted from her upper jaw. That explained the vampire-like bites on the victims.

With a shriek, the demon girl flew at Mick, fingers curved like she had every intention of taking his eyes out. Mick caught her arm, using her momentum to fling her to the side. She hit the ground and tumbled beneath the kiddie slide.

Faster than anyone would ever believe, Zoe wiggled out from underneath the slide. She lashed out at Mick, kicking him in the shins. He grabbed her and slammed her to the ground, but Zoe was resilient and strong. The minute she hit the earth, she rolled, knocking Mick's feet out from under him.

He returned the favor and Zoe hit the ground so hard it made me wince. With hardly a pause, Zoe rolled over and grabbed Mick by the hair, slamming his head into the ground hard enough to do some serious damage.

"Mick!" I ran toward them, fear lending me speed.

Zoe took off running again. I hesitated between helping Mick and going after the demon.

"Don't just stand there. Get her." Mick's voice was a little strained, but at least he was all right. With a nod, I took off after the girl.

She was much faster than me. I knew there was no way I'd be able to keep up with her for long. I quickly scanned the ground for anything useful. I smiled as I spotted just the right thing, pausing to scoop it up.

She was several feet ahead of me when I threw the baseball- sized rock. It smacked into the back of her skull, taking her down hard.

I dashed the last few steps, leaping onto her back. She fought like a wild cat, clawing and kicking, but she was still weak, stunned from the blow, and I had the slightest advantage.

Wrapping one arm around Zoe's throat, I squeezed, cutting off the other girl's airway. At first she struggled so hard she nearly threw me off, but soon her body began to weaken and her movements turned sluggish. Her squeaky little sounds as she struggled for air made me feel physically ill, but this was a necessary evil. She had to be stopped.

Finally she fell still, unconscious from lack of oxygen. With Zoe no longer fighting me, I was able to get a better grip. Memories faded in and out, fuzzy but growing stronger. I knew what I had to do to stop her.

I closed my eyes, taking in a deep breath. I wasn't sure I could do this, but I had no choice. I reached out and wrapped my hand around the rock I'd just thrown.

Putting my entire body weight into it, I smashed the rock into the demon girl's temple. She would recover. Eventually. Her demon half made her nearly immortal. But for now we wouldn't have to keep fighting her. There was no other way Mick and I could contain her.

I slowly climbed to her feet, my entire body aching as I fought back wave after wave of nausea. I realized I was fighting a losing battle, so I ran for the bushes, heaving up everything in my stomach until there was only bile. Shakily, I wiped my mouth, wishing I had some gum or something. I felt Mick's presence behind me.

"She hurt you."

"I'm fine."

"You're bleeding, babe."

"What?" I glanced up at Mick and then down at myself. I couldn't see any blood.

"Here." He gently swiped his thumb across my cheek coming away with a smear of blood.

I touched my face. Sure enough, there were long furrows there from where Zoe must have scratched me. "I didn't even feel it."

"Adrenaline will do that to you." He pulled out a tin of mints from his pocket, giving me an apologetic smile as he handed them over. I took them with a nod of thanks. Couldn't exactly blame him. My breath smelled gross, even to myself.

He stared down at the still form. "You killed her." There was no inflection in his tone to indicate how he felt. Was he angry? Did he blame me?

"Only temporarily," I assured him. "She'll be fine. It'll take a while. A couple hours maybe. Her body will heal and she'll wake up."

"Wait a minute, why didn't you mention this little factoid earlier? Could have saved us a hell of a lot of trouble." Now he definitely looked angry and I couldn't blame him.

"Uh, not exactly." I had no idea how to explain without sounding like I needed a mental health assessment. "I'll tell you about it later, okay? Right now we need to find a place to keep her before she wakes up."

"So we stash her some place and then what? She's dangerous. We can't let her go. And can you imagine what the cops would say if we tried to explain it to them?"

"You're right, we can't let her go. We need to turn her over to the local hunter." The one who still hadn't called me back.

"She's in France at the moment."

I glanced up at him, startled. "You know Morgan Bailey?" Apparently there was a lot more to Mick Egan that I'd realized. It also explained why he had been completely unfazed by my talk of demons and vampires.

"Yeah. She's a friend. How do you know her?"

"Long story." One I wasn't about to go into right then. "We'll need to hold Zoe until Morgan gets back, then we can turn her over."

"How do you suggest we do that?"

I smiled. There was something else I'd remembered. Something witches the world over had used for centuries. "Magic."

CHAPTER FOURTEEN

Before we left the park, I gave Liz a quick call. Leaving the janitor's body lying in the middle of the hallway for teachers and students to find whenever they opened the school again was not an option. I probably should have called the cops, but they'd be able to trace the call and there would be all kinds of awkward questions. For all Liz's faults, she cared about my safety and she'd no doubt tell the police she'd been the one to find the body.

"Abbie, what on earth were you doing at the school in the middle of the night?" Her tone was snippy, but underneath I could hear relief that I was okay.

"It's not that late. I forgot one of my books and I knew the janitor would let me in. I didn't expect anything bad to happen." It was lame, but it was just the sort of thing a human teenager might do, if she happened to be the principal's niece.

"Did you see...anyone?"

"No," I assured her. "He let me in, I got my books, I went to find him. And I did. I just...I ran. I'm sorry, Aunt Liz. I should have stayed. I should have called the cops."

"No. No. You did the right thing. Don't tell anyone about this, okay?" Her voice was firm.

"Okay, Aunt Liz." I gave a fake sniffle just for good measure. "But the police..."

"I'll leave work early and take care of it. You just go home." She hung up. Maybe she thought I'd argue. I wouldn't have.

I slid the phone into my pocket and gave Mick a smile. "She took the bait."

"Good. Now let's go practice some magic."

# # #

"This is creepy." Mick shoved his hands in his pockets as he glanced around the old crypt. It sounded like he was enjoying the experience. "Are you sure sticking her in a public cemetery is a good idea? Won't someone find her?"

"Not until we want them to." There was no place I knew of in this city that would be safe to hold a demon until the hunter returned, but I knew things that most people didn't. Like the fact that there were little pockets between our world and the next. Places were things could be stored. Places where things could never escape. All it took was a little knowledge of how to use those places, and the djinn had that knowledge.

After my conversation with Liz, Mick had vanished, only to show up with a car a few minutes later. I hadn't even known he owned a car. We'd shoved the sort-of-dead demon in the car and headed to my house to collect supplies. Liz would be gone awhile dealing with cops and whatever else, so we were able to head

Fearless

immediately for the nearest cemetery with above ground crypts.

Zoe, still unconscious and covered in blood, lay on top of the sarcophagus in the middle of the crypt. It was the oldest grave in the shared tomb and as such held the most residual power, the closest connection to the other side.

Mick watched me closely as I placed white candles around the demon girl's body at just the right intervals. Then I sprinkled a line of salt in a circle around the sarcophagus and me. The circle would protect the outside world from whatever happened inside. It would not, however, protect me from the demon.

Finally, I dipped my finger in some plain old cooking oil and painted an ancient djinn symbol on Zoe's forehead. It would keep her still and cooperative. More or less.

They were all useless, actually, all these little rituals. They did nothing in and of themselves, but without direct access to my djinn energy, I needed them to help me focus on what did work: manipulating universal energy.

"Wait." Mick stepped toward me, but did not cross the line. I'd explained to him how dangerous that could be. "She's waking up."

"I know. I need her to wake up if we're to find out what happened." And we needed to know the truth. Or at least I did.

"She's dangerous, Zip."

91

I gave him my sunniest smile. "And so am I."

Before he could utter another word I began the ritual, closing up the circle around myself and the demon girl. Power flared along the salt line. I could sense it, but not as I would have done in my djinni form.

"The circle is in place. You will be able to see and hear us, but you won't be able to cross the line."

Mick nodded, his eyes a little wide. Apparently he could feel the energy, too. It was a nice change from all the humans who seemed completely magic-blind.

I traced lines through the air over Zoe's body, murmuring in the language of my ancestors. I pulled down energy into the lines, forming a cage around her, invisible to the human eye. Once that was complete, I stepped closer.

"Zoe."

Her eyes opened, staring up at me. She appeared a little calmer, which was good. It meant the magic was working.

"Hi, there." I kept my voice gentle and even. "Remember me?"

Zoe stared at me blankly. Then comprehension flooded her face. "Zip." Her voice was scratchy as if she hadn't used it much lately. No doubt that was true.

"That's right. Zip Roberts. How are you feeling?"

The other girl seemed to mull that over for a while. "Better. I think. More...myself."

I smiled. "I bet. Do you know what happened to you?"

Zoe shook her head. "No." She seemed agitated, either by the question or her own lack of knowledge.

"Do you remember what you did?"

That seemed to agitate her even more. She twisted against her invisible bonds. "I don't want to."

"That's okay," I soothed. "Take your time. But you need to say it."

"I...I killed people." Zoe said, eyes downcast. Tears slid from the corners of her eyes, tracking their way down her cheeks.

"Yes."

"I don't understand why." Her chest heaved on a sob. "I didn't want to hurt anyone."

"It's because of what you are."

Her eyes were wide. "What do you mean?"

"Zoe, you're half demon."

She stared at me, face white, her whole body shaking. "No. *Nononono*." But I could tell by the look in her eyes that she knew the truth.

"When did the change start?"

Sobs wracked her so hard now she could hardly speak. "Six months ago."

"But you didn't start attacking people until a couple weeks ago."

"A-a-animals."

Somehow she'd manage to control her demon rage long enough to avoid killing humans, feeding her bloodlust instead with animals. That had to have taken some serious will-power.

"But eventually they weren't enough, and you couldn't control the urges anymore."

Zoe nodded, her entire body exuding misery. "But every time, I would feel so guilty, I couldn't eat. I just got hungrier and hungrier." She shuddered. "And angrier."

It made total, awful sense. Her demon half was clearly a blood demon. A Strix, maybe. I glanced up at Mick whose expression was grim. "But why did you use the knife? Cut their throats?"

"Because I had to hide the marks. No one could know."

"But those people, Zoe. Why did you choose those people?" I figured it was because they were available at the time, but her answer surprised me.

Zoe let out a small sigh. "It was better."

"Better?" What on earth was she talking about?

"People laughed at them. Made fun of them. Beat them up."

"They were all bullied," I said.

"Yes." That single word said it all. Zoe had been bullied, too. Before she changed. "They were in pain. So much pain. I wanted to help them."

"But how did killing them make it better? How did you help them?" I had a bad feeling I already knew the answer.

A smile, almost angelic in its beauty, spread across Zoe's blood smeared face.

"I freed them."

CHAPTER FIFTEEN

I exchanged glances with Mick. He gave a little nod as if to say he was with me. There was nothing left for me to do except stick Zoe in a place where she couldn't hurt anyone else.

"What are you going to do to me?" Zoe whimpered. Her face was a mess of tears, snot, and blood. Where she was going, it wouldn't matter.

I placed my hands over her, palms down, one above her forehead and above her sternum. Focusing on the nearest candle flame I began chanting. Meaningless in and of itself, like the other magical apparatus, but useful for focusing my internal energy.

"What are you doing?" The demon girl was practically shrieking now, fighting violently against the invisible ropes that tied her to the top of the sarcophagus. I didn't bother telling her it was useless.

I visualized a portal opening up beneath my hands, right over Zoe's body. I imagined her sliding into the pocket that existed between this world and the others, out of sync with any of them. Like a secret room in an old castle. There, but not.

I heard Mick gasp and opened my eyes. Beneath my hands shimmered a bright light, oval in shape, covering Zoe's body. She stared at me with wide, frightened eyes. I steeled my nerves, forcing myself not to feel sorry for her. Granted, the change and its resulting violence hadn't been her fault, but allowing her to roam free wasn't an option. The violence would only escalate. It was her nature.

I had no choice. I had to do what must be done. I had to be fearless.

"Please, please, please." She was sobbing, begging so hard her words were almost incomprehensible.

I gave a gentle push with my mind and the light engulfed her. Zoe screamed, though I knew she felt no pain, only fear. And then between one heartbeat and the next she was gone.

# # #

"She's really going to be okay?"

I was glad Mick was concerned about Zoe. He didn't hate her because of what she'd done. He understood she wasn't in control

"She will be fine. She will basically be asleep the entire time. Sort of like being in stasis. Safe until the hunter is available to deal with her."

"Morgan will do the right thing." He sounded sure. As if he knew from experience. One day he would tell me his story. As I would tell him mine. But not today.

I nodded. "Yes. She always does."

The walk home was at once awkward and weirdly exhilarating. If I were honest with myself, I had to admit I enjoyed Mick's company. I liked the way he made me feel.

"Well, this is it," I said cheerfully once we'd reached the front door. "Thanks for the escort. And for the help with, you know. Everything." Gods, could I be any more stupid?

A little half smile quirked his full lips. For the longest time he didn't say anything. Then he reached out. I felt myself sway toward him just a little.

Mick traced my jaw line with one finger. His touch was exquisitely gentle, sending sparks zinging through my blood stream. I fought to keep still. To not let him see how he was effecting me.

He leaned in so close I thought he was going to kiss me. My breath caught in my throat. Part of me desperately wanted that kiss. Wanted it so much I thought I'd die of wanting. Or more embarrassingly, grab him and hold on for dear life.

He didn't kiss me. At first. Instead his lips skimmed my ear sending shivers through my body.

And then his lips were on mine. Soft and velvety and oh, so sweet. Giving, taking, demanding.

My hands skimmed his chest and curled over his shoulders as he took the kiss deeper, plundering my mouth with his tongue. My whole body was on fire. Yearning for more of him.

And then he pulled away, leaving me stunned. Bereft.

"Maybe one day," he said, voice low and husky, "you'll find a way to let me in."

I knew he didn't mean physically. "Maybe."

He gave me that wry little half smile that made my heart lurch. Then he turned and strode across the porch and down the steps, disappearing into the night.

I watched him go, blood still singing from his touch. I touched lips that still tingled from his kiss.

"One day."

The End

About Shéa MacLeod

Shéa MacLeod is the author of urban fantasy post-apocalyptic sci-fi paranormal romance with a twist of steampunk. She has dreamed of writing novels since before she could a crayon. She totally blames her mother.

After a six year sojourn in London, England, a dearth of good donuts has driven her back to her hometown. She now resides in the leafy green hills outside of Portland, where she indulges in her fondness for strong coffee, Ancient Aliens reruns, lemon curd, and dragons.

Shéa MacLeod

Other Books by Shéa MacLeod

Sunwalker

Kissed by Darkness
Kissed by Fire
Kissed by Smoke
Kissed by Moonlight- October 2013

Dragon Wars

Dragon Warrior
Dragon Lord
Dragon Goddess

Cupcake Goddess Novelettes

Be Careful What You Wish For
Nothing Tastes As Good

Sign up for Shéa MacLeod's mailing list at
http://sheamacleod.com/mailing-list-2/ and be the first
to hear about new releases